A GRAY
VOYAGER

A NOVEL OF SELF DISCOVERY

A Gray Voyager

A Novel of Self Discovery

Daniel Hill Zafren

Published by Time Treasures Books, Goose Creek, South Carolina
www.timetreasuresbooks.com

ISBN: 978-0-9833042-9-6

Printed in the United States of America

Cover and interior by Susan Newman Design Inc.

The earlier books by Daniel Hill Zafren:

In a World We Never Made (2001)
A Door Never Opened (2003)
Shadow Selves (2005)
Network of Death (2006)
Not Lost – Just Not Found (2008)
Restless Beauty (2009)
Glimpses of Forgotten Dreams (2010)
Echo in the Heart (2011)
Double Hugs (2011)
Page Passage (2013)
Wish Winds (2014)
Unfinished Thinking (2015)
Vain Regrets (2016)
Network Secret (2016)
Forever Old, Forever New (2017)
Endless Time (2018)

And thou, gray voyager to the breezeless sea
Of infinite Oblivion – speed thou on;
Another gift of time succeedith thee
Fresh from the hand of God; for thou hast done
The errand of thy destiny; and none
May dream of thy returning. Go and bear
Mortality's frail records to thy cold,
Eternal prison-house; the midnight prayer
Of suffering bosoms, and the fevered care
Of wordly hearts; the miser's dream of gold;
Ambition's grasp at greatness; the quenched
     light
Of broken spirits; the forgiven wrong
And the abiding curse – ay, bear along
These wrecks of thy own making. Lo, thy knell
Gathers upon the windy breath of night,
Its last and faintest echo. Fare thee well!

— John Greenleaf Whittier

The Zest of Life

Henry van Dyke

Let me live my life from year to year,
With forward face and unreluctant soul;
Not hastening to, nor turning from the goal;
Not mourning for the things that disappear
In the dim past, nor holding back in fear
From what the future veils; but with a whole
and happy heart, that pays its toll
To Youth and Age, and travels on with cheer.

So let the way wind up the hill or down,
O'er rough or smooth, the journey will be joy:
Still seeking what I sought when but a boy,
New friendship, high adventure, and a crown,
My heart will keep the courage of the quest,
And hope the road's last turn will be the best.

BOOK ONE

THE SEARCH

PREFACE

How do you search for your future? The future is a great unknown. It does not happen on its own in regard to what you want to do or where you want to be. Many internal and external factors can make the shaping of destiny difficult and even painful. Young people deceive themselves in believing that options will develop along the way. Sometimes they do; most often not. The elderly are also concerned about their future, and they are astute enough to know that many of the options they could have taken advantage of have already passed them by. However, just because a future may be limited by time and space, that does not mean the search is any less important.

An old person seeking the future can be called a gray voyager. As an analogy, the quest can be likened to a hot air balloon ride hovering close to the landscape of life as it glides by. At times, it is close enough so details of the features that are passed by can be noted, and at other times more distant so that things are obscure or not totally defined. All along, it is unknown what surrounding conditions might be. The flight can be through a calm sky, or it may hit sudden storms or other turbulence. Unanticipated winds may blow the balloon off a desired course. The gray voyager may be relaxed and enthralled by the vista. Or, the voyager may become wary and fear may dictate holding on tightly.

Sustained by memories and experiences, a gray voyager tries to find a path as direct as possible to a destination that may exist only in the mind or heart. It is just one more struggle an old person must endure. Yet, the poignant lyrics in a song from the musical

South Pacific bear deliberation. "You have to have a dream. If you don't have a dream, how do you expect a dream to come true?"

How should an author create the search for the future of a gray voyager? At first blush, it might seem simple, far easier than a real person's task. Yet, it is not that facile. If the author simulates an actual situation, then all of the practical struggles need to be balanced with a host of theoretical ones, all the while portraying believable actions and emotions. If the author first decides, among a myriad of possibilities both good and bad, what that future might or should be, filling in the blanks on the path to that future can be challenging. Which memories and experiences, real or imaginary, are most compelling? What other characters or events might be influential, in whole or in part? With happenstance removed from the equation, all must stem entirely from the author's pen.

ONE

The vagaries of life are easier to describe than to understand. They can run the full gamut from remarkable to ordinary to dismal. That is just what he would tell his students whenever there was a welcome digression from the strict course structure that the law school imposed. He was sure the students greeted any side track as valuable as the maxims of law digested. The ensuing questions and discussions verified what is well known – experience can be as useful as book knowledge, if not more so.

Isaac Denton decided on the day after his eightieth birthday to examine all of those vagaries. The day of his birthday would not have been a good time for introspection as the day was nearly consumed by the party his wife, Clara, had held at the house with all of the children and grandchildren in attendance. He would rather have had a peaceful day, but the family wanted to celebrate the occasion and he was not able to think of a good enough reason to justify any denial. It probably was a milestone to mark as his parents and siblings had not lived that long.

So, where does one start looking back on a life spanning eighty chronological years and yet encompassing longer than that because it has been an entire lifetime? The first memory as a child would seem to be as good a starting point as any. There is a definite problem with memories, however. Does the memory hold more or less than what actually happened? To what degree when looking back does the present affect its interpretation? Does that embellish or detract from the actual occurrence? And, how would one even begin to know the difference?

Then, too, he was at a loss as to what would be classified as the first actual memory. There were earlier snippets in the mind recalling laughing or crying, a parental hug, a brother's shove, and a sister's pat on the cheek. So, it had to be his substantial involvement in the event. If that was the criteria, there were two things he remembered clearly, although he was not sure which one was the earlier in time. He was also not sure which one had greater significance at the time or even if he could judge it as of today.

His childhood was spent on the streets of Brooklyn. The family lived in a two-bedroom apartment on the third floor of an old building with dark and dingy hallways, smells intermingled from whatever was cooking behind doors and mold and mildew hidden in crevices. He and his brother slept in one bedroom, his sister in the other, while the parents slept on a convertible sofa in what would otherwise have been the dining area. They ate at a table in an alcove off of the kitchen.

One of the memories took place in the country, and perhaps just the change in the environment added to the impact of the event. There was a meadow and no tall buildings as in the city, just a row of cottages bordering the meadow. It was very hot. He was barely able to walk on his own, and his father led him over to a metal contraption which he was later told was a well. His father took hold of the lever and pumped it several times and cold water gushed out of the spout. It was magic to a little tyke. He put his face under the spout and his father pumped again. The cold water spilled over his face and into his open mouth. Then, his father helped him to pump the lever and he laughed as the water ushered forth. His clothes did not get wet as he was not wearing any. His father was not wearing any either. They were at a nudist colony. In the late 1930s and early 1940s nudism was touted as healthy physically and emotionally for families, and nudist camps were fairly popular. It represented acceptance of what was completely natural. Too bad all that has been lost in the shuffle of modern times, along with artificial and unnecessary restricted morals imposed by a staid society.

The other early memory was with the entire family listening to the radio. It was well before the days of television, and after dinner the family would gather around and listen to the radio. At the earliest time he could recall the event in its entirety, he was sitting on the floor playing with some clothespins. His mother, Jean, was sitting in a rocking chair knitting. His father, Albert, was sitting in one of the easy chairs reading the newspaper. Francine, his older sister, was also sitting on the floor reading a magazine. Jacob, his older brother, was laying on his back on the floor and his eyes were closed. Izzy, and that is what everyone called him, all of a sudden started questioning things in his mind. How could a wooden box talk or play music? Why was this his family and not the Epsons who lived directly across the hall? There were no answers for him to dwell on, but it was the first instance he could recall that involved his introduction to the ability and necessity of questioning things. The thinking never stopped after that. Even to this day when his mind should be slowing down he rarely accepted things as they appeared to be. His mind would jump to other alternatives, other reasons for what might not appear so obvious. That is why he was never a truly contented man. How could anyone be content on the road of life when what may lie beyond the next bend is unknown?

There were many other childhood memories, some clearer than others. Some, as he dwelled upon them, more meaningful than others. His mother played the piano. There was a small spinet in the living room. Often he would sit at her feet and watch her slender fingers caress the keys. It fascinated him. He tried learning to play but he had no musical talent. He should have since his grandfather played the french horn with the Philharmonic Orchestra. Jacob played the guitar well and Francine was adept at the oboe.

A neighbor down the hall collapsed on the stairs and died. It was the first time he saw a dead body. The concept of death was new to him and he was not sure he grasped all of the nuances. He was no stranger to death later on in life as his parents both died from cancer, Jacob succumbed to a heart attack, and Francine was killed in a horrific accident. His own death dangled before him, and he was still perplexed by its finality. All expectations, thoughts, and dreams gone as if in a puff of smoke.

Being a lawyer, one would think that over all of the years he could make a strong case for his contentment. Maybe, because he was a lawyer, the case was not strong enough, not overly convincing for his inner being. So, if one were to ask him if he was happy, his truthful response would be that he was satisfied but not contented. Or, was that merely a distinction without a difference?

Two

For the kind of mental examination he was engaged in, he not only expected numerous interruptions he also anticipated it would take some time. It might take weeks or even months, and that might be just the first swipe. Certain glimpses into the past might need a revisit. As Whittier so aptly phrased it, Izzy would have to closely scrutinize the wrecks of his own making. There was no reason to rush any of it as he needed to prepare for wherever the gray voyager might wind up.

It was a warm Spring day. Clara made a salad lunch that they had on the screened-in back porch where their three yorkshire terriers could scamper around or find a sunny spot to lie in. They did not talk much these days, but he figured after being married for fifty-four years on top of a form of extended courtship, they had already said to one another all that needed to be said. One of the shocks that might come at the end of this thinking would be that he might indeed have something new to say.

He studied Clara as she ate, and he did consider himself lucky to have had such an amiable lifetime partner. She had supported him in all of his endeavors, even those that ran beyond conventional limits. As an exemplary mother, he concluded he was truly blessed. He had hoped he had been half the husband as the wife she had been, and half the father as well to their son and two daughters. There would be lots more thinking about her later on no doubt.

After lunch, he lingered on the porch and dozed with one

of the yorkies curled up on his lap. Retirement was yet another gift that life bestows on those fortunate enough to be able to do so. There are no fixed schedules, no set agendas. In effect, every day is a weekend day.

Once back on his mental journey, his childhood was dominated by two pervasive influences. One was the marriage of his parents, which was unusual and controversial at the time. His father was Jewish and his mother a Catholic. They were bound together as society frowned on their union. Their respective families ignored them, although that softened with a reluctant acceptance when Jacob was born. Izzy celebrated the Jewish holidays as well as Christmas and Easter with the families. He liked that, particularly getting presents at Hanukkah and Christmas. It was not a strain to touch both worlds, and the older he got the more he realized he was the beneficiary of some larger life lessons. Anyway, he was able to see throughout his growing period an exceptional love between a man and a woman. Devotion brings respect, affection, and tender consideration. Children thrive in such an atmosphere.

The other influence was being an active participant in street life. A mix of constant diverse activities, many people of various ages, races, and cultures, and with all sorts of noises and sounds ranging from melodic to harsh, leads to keen observation and tempered reaction. Being attentive and receptive to it all was the way to know what was happening, and what was about to happen. On the avenue where the stores were, he knew every store's secrets and employees. He knew when it was the best time to go in one, whether to get a free sample or an insight on what was going on behind closed doors. His favorite store was Herron's Bakery, not only because he could get a free wedge of pumpernickel raisin bread from the loaf that was usually on the counter, but pretty Janice Ruffies who had a gigantic bosom worked there. She would hug him each time he would go in as she thought he was so cute and his face would be mashed into those monster orbs. The street was the place to learn from the older children and to pass it on to the younger ones. It was the place to try what you might otherwise not dare to try, when was the best time to try it, and how not to get caught. The street was the place where you heard each and every rumor, and knew which family was going through an upheaval or a bonanza. One learned about crime, sex, love, and friendship. Looking back, it was a never ending beehive of activity. You had to grow up fast and smart or be left behind.

School was a place to learn fundamentals, but one learned more just in the walk to and from the school with friends. Two of their favorite pastimes were identifying the make of the cars that passed them by and comparing notes on which of the girls was developing breasts the fastest. He was not a good student and got blamed for devilish antics whether he was involved or not. He lost count of how many chalk erasers he had clapped together and how many inkwells he had filled. His poor mother had to often scrub his clothes to get the ink stains out. He had the same teacher for all of the eight years in P.S. 99, and even though it was some seventy years ago he still remembered her name, Mrs. Fletcher. Until she went to her grave, he was sure she remembered his name. He had often joked that the only way he proceeded from grade to grade was the incentive for her to finally get rid of him.

In high school, things were different. He actually became a good student and discovered the joy of learning things that he had thought about and which he then knew he was curious about. He also had to take a city bus to the high school, and it was generally crowded with other students as well as working folk. It was on the bus that he met his first real girlfriend. He had never seen her before and she would get on two stops up the avenue. Her name was Linda Appleby, and she had short red hair and freckles. There would be no seats available and they would share the same pole as they stood. It was a month before he worked up enough courage to start speaking to her. Her coy smile should have told him that it was about time. She was one year ahead of him and they had no classes together, but they managed to meet in the lunch room and would pass in the halls with a warm smile and a knowing glance. They dated every Friday and Saturday night. Once a month when he would get his allowance, they would go to the movies. At other times, they hung out on the avenue or for a dime would ride the subway for hours. In the cold months, they would sit in the old lobby of his or her building. In the summers, people did not stay in their hot apartments as only the movie theater and the Chinese restaurant were air conditioned. People brought out chairs to set up on the sidewalks or they sat on the stoops. He and Linda would join the throng. She had an early curfew, so that did limit their time together. When he looked back on it, there were so many worthwhile conversations that they had. Young people do find a variety of subjects to expound on. A blend of enthusiasm and curiosity can foster deep probing. Gradually, they lost interest in each other, or maybe it was being distracted elsewhere. It was a pleasant memory of exploratory feelings in a much slower moving time. Slow moving times are gone forever.

THREE

Obligations and commitments led to numerous interruptions in the mental chronicles of a gray voyager. Once a week he was a volunteer in the meals on wheels program, delivering meals to incapacitated seniors who could not make it to the Senior Center for the meals served there. As long as his own physical condition was adequate, he wanted to help those less fortunate. One day a week he volunteered at the local university library where he probably did more reading than the chores he had agreed to help with. Then, of course, there were the activities of the grandchildren which he supported by attending when he could and cheering them on accordingly. Various sports and musical presentations were the usual fare. The granddaughters were as active as the grandsons, and he was conscious of not portraying any favorites, although he did not have one. Once a week he met his old friends, all retired now, for breakfast at Ginger's Hot Shoppe. Ginger was an ex-wife of a law professor he taught with, and she had confided in him during those trying times as she knew he had a sympathetic ear. When she opened the restaurant, she let the old men's breakfast group, which they called the Breakfast Club use a private back room so that they could be as raucous as they might want to be. It was a good thing it was only once a week because there might have been some medical alerts if it had been more often.

The grandest distraction from his mental sojourn was the

book he started to write two years ago.

Reflecting the anticipation of the current mental voyage, it was about the unexpected turn of events in an old man's life. He did not write on any schedule, just when the urge came over him. He might write a paragraph or a couple of pages, and he would write it out in longhand and then feed it into the computer in his study later. The study, which he referred to as his office, was the one place in the house that Clara had not decorated and which she often said was afraid to go into as a dust bunny might gobble her up.

He had no idea how close he was to completing the book. As with so many other things, there was no reason or incentive to rush to finish it. Even impending death might not urge it all to completion. Perhaps, the book was a kind of gray voyager's tale as well, and he had an inkling that at some point the two voyages might converge. Then, it might be that age old dilemma – is it life imitating art or art imitating life?

Amidst all of the goings on, he started to get up earlier than he used to. There was something peaceful and comforting in the early hours when he had the house and time to himself. He would have a pot of coffee, and then settle on the small sofa in the office with the yorkies stretched out beside him. It was conducive to pursue his mental trek.

In his senior year in high school, he still had no idea what sort of career path he would follow. His parents were frugal with their savings and his father's salary as a wholesale furniture salesman, so there were funds to send all of the children to college. Jacob had become an architect. Francine was halfway through a program at a teacher's college. His liberal father would not consider any choice of colleges in the South as he was opposed to segregation. Izzy wound up at the University of Buffalo, long before it became part of the State of New York university system. To this day, he still remembered the Alma Mater and would occasionally sing it when he was alone.

> *Where once the Indian trod the wintry wood,*
> *Where once the antlered deer have stood;*
> *Brothers, tonight we sing the chorus free*
> *Pledging our love to our University;*
> *To U. of B., to U. of B.*
> *Our Alma Mater by the inland sea.*

Being away from home and dorm life were eye-opening. Before the first week was over he had two girlfriends, Celia, a senior girl from the local high school when those senior girls invaded the campus and latched on to whatever freshman boy they could find, and Helene from the women's dorm on the other side of the quadrangle. With these initial distractions, it was hard to get in to a study routine. That all changed when the first snow arrived in late October and with lake effect snow continuing through March. All this was accompanied by fierce winds so that rope was strung along walkways for people to hold on to. With no place to go to and such difficult conditions, studying was just about the only thing to do.

It was in the spring that he had an experience that would have a tremendous impact on his life. Students at the University who lived in the city were called "townies." A townie girl, who was in a wheelchair, was in two of his classes. It was obvious that her legs were exceptionally thin and misshapen. He had not given much thought before that to people with disabilities or those who were discounted by society. One day, as one of the classes was ending and the other students rushed out of the room, he started talking to her, and it turned out to be one of the most memorable conversations he had ever had. She was bright, humorous, and extremely perceptive. As he gazed intently at her face, it struck him how very beautiful she was. Cheron Bertowsky was her name. He could never forget that as he could never forget her. Since it was lunch time, he offered to push her to the cafeteria so they could have lunch together. She had her own lunch from home, but accepted his invitation as she had an hour before her father was going to pick her up. For that hour there was no lull in the conversation, and he had decided before that hour was up that he was in love. He asked her out on a date, and that beautiful face blushed as she admitted she had never been asked out before. When he went to her house, her father let him take the family car for the outing. She was as light as a feather as he put her in the front seat and collapsed the wheelchair that went into the trunk. When he kissed her goodnight, it was not awkward. She cried as it was her first kiss. It was as natural an act as he could ever imagine, and each and every time he kissed her after that it was magical.

They spent all of their spare time together on school days, usually in the library or the Student Union. Holding hands was a favorite activity, and if he closed his eyes and let his inner spirit drift back to those days he could sense those warm dainty fingers entwined with his.

They dated every weekend until he went home for the summer. Due to a medical emergency at home, there was not enough money for him to go back in the fall, and he transferred to the City College of New York. He and Cheron exchanged letters and telephone calls for almost a year after that. It was the closeness to that exceptional woman that brought out a compassion in him that he had no idea he was capable of. He decided he wanted to become a lawyer and an advocate for the disabled, a class of persons who at that time had very limited rights. He could see it clearly now. He never loved anyone as deeply as he had loved Cheron, and had never, even with Clara, felt another person to be such a large part of himself. It probably was the kind of love his parents shared. He should have found a way to go back to Buffalo if for no other reason than to be with her. He should have married her, and in spite of the difficulties that might have been encountered he was sure he would have achieved the kind of happiness that he had never found elsewhere. There is no way to turn back the clock, no way to recapture the past. He also realized that no other woman had loved him as earnestly and genuinely as Cheron had. She loved him with her soul. He closed his eyes and his whole body shuddered. Just thinking of her made him fully alive.

FOUR

Introspection might be good for the mind but it is bad for the soul. Coming to the realization that this or that should have been done or that this or that should have been done in a different way brings forth a certain emotional agitation further adding to a basic unhappiness.

It took strict concentration and varying degrees of play acting to make sure no one else could tell he was entering a state of mental unrest. He had been introduced to play acting when in City College he tried out and obtained a part in *Death of a Salesman*. Acting is an escape route for the disenchanted. The inner being is masked by the character one pretends to become. Actors who proclaim to be creative and unrestrained also have a built in excuse to be different or pretend to be different. Unless one has has been to an acting group's party, there is little knowledge of how outlandish behavior can be glossed over by the fervor of the moment. His mind could grasp that in a memory, but his spirit had long since been so quieted that all he could do was to remember it.

An unanticipated major distraction occurred when their son, Brian, dropped in for a surprise visit and announced that he and his wife, Shelly, were getting a divorce. After nearly thirty years of marriage, their paths had grown apart and in an amiable agreement had decided to go their separate ways. Clara wept immediately. Actually, it did not come as a surprise to Izzy. He had noted for some time that there was a subtle aloofness in the marriage. It was more of a feeling than a knowing. He had made a point of not interfering in his children's adult lives. After all, he may be an expert in facets of the law but that was a far cry from being an expert in people's feelings and desires. He was only glad that the children of that marriage were no longer young so that there might be a modicum of order and stability in the forthcoming years. This is what he consoled Clara with, and yet he understood her anguish because of her consuming faith in the family as a unit. Their divergence in the philosophy of raising children had not been a bone of contention but it arose from time to time. Clara believed that it is best for a parent to give a child roots. Izzy believed wings are best.

Even though he was an attorney, he never handled a divorce case. For that matter, he had not been engaged in any criminal case or a host of other forms of legal disputes. Because of the guiding light that Cheron had inspired in him, right after passing the bar he went to work for a law firm specializing in civil rights cases. In that vast area he eventually carved out his desired niche as a defender for the disabled. It did not take long after that for his legal might to be felt and expounded on, leading to his spirited advocacy on their behalf before State and Federal legislatures. He gained national notoriety. That led to the offer from the law school to teach the newly added course on Law of the Disabled when it was added to the curriculum.

He was getting far ahead of himself here. Any professional accomplishments were not the genesis for his mental sojourn. He likened his gray voyage to a ride in a hot air balloon slowly drifting along the countryside, at times viewing the landscape from high above while at other times coming closer to the features that either interested him the most or deserved intense inspection.

While in college, the only interest beyond the studies was the theater productions. That is where he met Clara. She was an art major and participated in painting the scenery for the stage productions. At first, there was no romantic interest although she was extremely friendly and conversation was easy. His driving preoccupation was with the Library. He studied there most of the time, and he would often pursue research ventures totally unrelated to actual assignments. It is an awe-inspiring discovery that books are powerful tools to combat ignorance and absorb the lessons of history.

In their senior year, he and Clara dated a few times. She liked movies as much as he did, and they shared a particular enjoyment of Chinese food. She taught him how to use chopsticks, and that really did add to the essence of the occasions. The dates were pleasant, although not earth shaking. After graduation, Clara found a job clerking at a design firm and he went to a law school in the city. They dated at random times, and she was quite understanding of his study demands. It was in his final year when both his parents died three months apart, his mother from stomach cancer and his father from lung cancer, that Clara displayed the emotional support that truly endeared her to him. She was sensitive to his moods and feelings, and her genuine caring nature placated his worst fears. Between that and her pleasant demeanor and soft-spoken mannerism, he decided he loved her and that she would be an ideal life partner. Her most captivating feature, one which to even this day held him in complete awe, and was nearly hypnotized by it, was that she always appeared to be smiling. So many people display a form of sour harshness or bitterness on their faces, but Clara was almost angelic. They became engaged and planned to marry as soon as he passed the bar and landed his first job.

The wedding was a modest affair that they paid for

themselves, attended only by relatives and close friends. Of course, only Chinese food was served and that alone made it unique. They postponed a honeymoon, not knowing at the time that some twenty years would pass before they took a trip that might be classifiable as a honeymoon. Neither had any particular desire to travel, so it was not a major sacrifice. The marriage was launched, and the togetherness felt natural. It felt right. Time proved it to be so.

FIVE

As he settled on the office sofa one stormy morning, one of the yorkies, terrified of thunder, crawled behind him. He knew he had to face one of his own storms, one of the major obstacles in his sojourn. He did not have to convince himself that the marriage to Clara was good and lasting. If he equated comfort and placidity to love then he truly loved her. But, was that enough? There was not the passion, the yearning that he had felt briefly with Cheron. How important was that? Did a person rightfully deserve to be on a quest to find and hold on to only that? Or, does the complexity of love realistically lead to accept and bask in the pleasures and security of feelings warm and convenient? Does the soul make peace with what it has found or should there be no peace without every possible exploration being undertaken? Perhaps, Brian was a younger version of himself. Izzy, at age eighty, might not be able to adequately deal with a conclusion that he did not really love Clara and should now seek love out. Undoubtedly, even if possible, it might not be the utopia it represents. What could he do with and about it? In the meantime it would devastate Clara. Can he do that to her? He had better postpone this tangential trip until the rest of his life was placed in due context. However, would it not be amazing if after living mainly a practical life he might be transformed into a dreamer?

There had been moments and discussions over the children's growing years about moving out of the city. The city had so much to offer, such as off Broadway plays, concerts, dance festivals, that they basically enjoyed living there. As Clara perfected Chinese cooking at home, restaurants did not have the same appeal as in earlier days. The rent controlled apartment was adequate for the growing family, and there were so many activities for children that there was usually a choice of events to take them to. Private schooling was expensive, but there were so many other compensations. Then, too, he often had to work late and there were no commuting problems. He figured he saved at least two hours a day not having to commute. That does add up.

They did move to their current house in the suburbs when Izzy started teaching at the law school which was also outside the city. Having extra rooms, flowers, and trees, were a change that they grew accustomed to quickly enough. The children were still at home, and the change was good for them as well. Once the children were away at college, the extra rooms were for roaming until holidays when the house would be bustling.

Many of those years were now a blur in his mind, and he knew he had to come to terms with the significance of that. He remembered more about his students, particularly those he anticipated would go on to do exceptional deeds, then he did about his own children and home life. Of course, if he concentrated intently he might recall birthday parties, graduations, weddings, Thanksgiving feasts, and a host of other events. Once again, was he making it more of an issue than it was? Teaching was a different attention device than the easy going carefree participation in the household schedules and activities. Yet, he knew he had talked to Brian about the birds and bees when he was thirteen, but he could not remember it very well or even how he approached it. Clara had briefed the girls accordingly. He could not remember reading stories at bedtime, special shopping trips, or just having a casual conversation. Are family memories so superficial that they become obscured by the dust of time? Or, are they more in the heart than in the mind? Does every gray voyager merely accept the unfathomable because it has no bottom?

It was becoming clear to him that there are instances when direction and speed of the hot air balloon are out of control and may present unanticipated dangers. It then remains to be seen whether or not the trip is even worthwhile.

SIX

It had been a long and tiring day. The loving daughters, Jenny and Nadine, came over together mainly to console their mother about Brian's news. It was probably natural that when a marriage of a family member is in jeopardy the others tend to focus on their own marriages and question how things are going. That is not necessarily a bad thing, although it coats the entire picture with what Izzy calls unnecessary and unjustified fluff.

In the course of the discussion, in which Izzy was more of a listener than a participant, the daughters offered some problems in their own marriages. Clara was patient and encouraging, stating her usual sage counsel of making greater efforts at compromise and togetherness. She offered to come and stay with the grandchildren if the parents wanted to get away for some alone time. The modern world is more of a strain on families than in past times. Tell tale signs are everywhere. Modern families will never know the slow moving events of past eras when people could easily catch their breaths and luxuriate in the simple things. Back then, choices, if there were any, were uncomplicated. The gadgets of today which rule the wheres, whens, and hows, remove the human element from the equation, and the now need and availability of instant gratification fosters impatience and intolerance.

After the daughters left, Clara embraced him warmly. "I don't know what more to do."

His answer was what he knew she wanted to hear. "There

is nothing more you can do. If corrections to their lives have to be made, they need to make them."

"I just hate to see them frustrated and unhappy. Happiness can be such a simple thing."

"It is a state of mind, and the mind is never simple." That remark was more for him than for her.

"It really takes so little to be happy."

"We know that. They have to learn that for themselves. The real problem is that there are far too many distractions in the learning process."

"But you would think they saw that for themselves growing up in a loving and happy family."

"Seeing is not necessarily believing or a road to emulation."

"You are awfully negative today."

"I'm just echoing all that you heard from our children."

"You do believe things will get better, don't you?"

He took a moment to respond. What he said was again for her. "I hope so."

Izzy took to the teaching in the law school as the proverbial duck takes to water, although the first year was a trying period. Preparing for first-time lectures and seminars, and devising examinations was strenuous and time-consuming. The deaths of Jacob and Francine two months apart during that first year added a particular hardship. Jacob, who had been a fine specimen of health and strength, had a fatal heart attack. His wife and two children were ill-equipped and ill-informed as to what to do and how to handle the emotional and financial upheaval. Jacob did not have his affairs in order, apparently because he saw no need to plan for an early demise. Izzy spent time cementing that family's world together. Francine died instantly in a fiery car crash. Izzy shuddered each time he visualized that tragedy. She had no husband and family, and in his mind he could still hear her students at the school she was teaching at crying during the memorial service held for her there. Francine had been a loving sister, and he had always admired her intelligence and tenacity. At her death, he regretted deeply that he had not been in more frequent contact with her. The last time he had seen her was at Jacob's memorial, and it had probably been six months before that when they had lunch together. She had scant contact with Jacob and his family. As he thought about it now, she was probably lonely and felt detached from the family. As with so many other instances inherent in the fragility of life, he should have done more for her, been there more for her. It was also a sad realization that he was the last surviving member of his family. What would happen to the memories of that family after he was gone? Francine had possession of the family photo album as far as he knew, but when he had gone to her home to sort things out it was nowhere to be found. He had been in an antiques store once and he saw there a bunch of family albums that had gone unclaimed for one reason or another and were now for sale for a meager amount. Memories on a junk heap.

The second and ensuing years at the law school were easier. He was able to adopt and expand on all the work of the first year. That left him more time and a greater inclination to interact and inspire his students to make further inroads in the civil rights field after graduation. The road to personal freedoms was long and winding with many pitfalls along the way. It was gratifying when former students contacted him about their accomplishments. It was as if an extension of himself was still out there making paths in the wilderness.

The conclusion he drew from it all was that he had led a full and productive life. It had also been a healthy one. He had never had a stay in a hospital, no accidents or major diseases or illnesses. The only medical oddity he had experienced was when he was bitten by a bat. Soon after moving to the house, one day just before sunrise he had taken the dogs out into the backyard. Either the bat swooped down and bit him on the forearm or he had raised his arm up directly into the bat's flight path. He had undergone the series of rabies shots and apparently had no after effects, although he would joke that since then he salivated more profusely. Now, he had been bitten not by the wanderlust bug but by the wonderlust bug. He feared that might have serious repercussions.

SEVEN

Just because he had reached what might be described as a tentative conclusion, that did not mean that the survey of his life was over. More from his past had to be added to the quest, and greater details of what he remembered the most needed to be brought to light. In retrospect, the transitions were important as well.

As he reread what he had written in his book so far to make sure there was no confusion or inconsistencies with the story or characters, he was a bit surprised, although he should not have been, that some of the experiences and past lives of the characters were replicas or variations of his own. The main character, Aaron Comstock, the old man revisiting his life to make sense of where he was and where he should be going, had memories embellishing his own or experiences touched by his own involvement in the past. On the other hand, an entire chapter was devoted to Aaron's relationship with his college sweetheart, Renee. There had been no Renee in Izzy's life, but there was no denying she represented Cheron and other women he had been with as well as a projection back to what the right girlfriend might have been based on his current outlook. More than that, she symbolized what would have been the ideal if he had wished it so. Too bad life is rarely what one wishes it to be.

Aaron had met Renee on the college bus trip for students who wanted to participate in a civil rights march in Washington,

D.C. As it was late in the evening, they were all tired as they boarded the bus for the trip back. Aaron grabbed the first available seat, and it was next to Renee. He did not know her, but she sure knew him. It turned out that she had a secret crush on him. By the end of the ride home, they got to know each other well enough and she wound up sleeping with her head on his shoulder. After that, they were inseparable. He imparted his love of books to her, and she imbued her love of nature to him. In discovering their inner world, they explored facets of the outside world that neither had dared to experience alone.

He would not call it writer's block. It was just frustrating to realize he was veering off course. Rather than attempting to bring reality into clearer focus, his new found exposure as a dreamer was leading him to a state of what might have been rather than what actually was. Two entirely different kettles of fish! Maybe, he had to coast lower in the hot air balloon to get a better survey of the life landscape as he drifted by it.

He was never apprehensive about being old. Eighty might have seemed old when he was a youngster, but it was just a number. Whatever eighty was or was supposed to be, he felt good and had control of his being both physically and mentally. He was realistic to know that any of this could change quickly and perhaps without any warning. It might call for an adjustment in his outlook, his routine, and in the execution of his desires, although he would meet such a happening head on. He would dread not having full mental capacity, yet such would only be an obstacle to be dealt with. And, if the point was ever reached where he no longer had any quality of life, he had already made preparations for that. He had not needed friends in high places, just in the right places. One of his oldest friends, Howard Jansky, was a physician and had been Izzy's primary doctor since Howard started his practice in internal medicine. Now retired, his daughter, Eissen, was also a doctor. Both were well versed in his final wishes if an empty cause arose and they were prepared to ease his way. That was of great comfort. Clara also knew of this and would contact them if he was unable to do so himself. There was the same arrangement for her.

Izzy met Howard when he was nineteen. That summer he had obtained a job as a counselor at a children's camp in Connecticut. There were six nine and ten year old boys in his bunk. Howard was a senior in a pre-med program at Cornell University and was the swimming instructor at the camp. He slept in Izzy's bunk and ate meals with them. The two became fast close friends, a basic shared philosophy of wanting to help people underlying a special bond. Howard was a bit shy with girls, and even though Izzy was a far cry from an expert, he helped foster a relationship with one of the female counselors who had a hankering for Howard. Howard had already been accepted to medical school, so it was his last summer of freedom and frolic.

The two men stayed in touch as careers advanced, and once Howard opened up his practice Izzy was among his first patients. A friendship matured as life swept them along, and as Izzy looked back on it since he had been relatively healthy he had probably given Howard more legal advice than he had received medical treatment. In any event, it was comforting having a person he trusted so completely as a medical advisor and confidant. Howard had long since given up his shyness with women. In fact, he wound up at the other end of the spectrum and had been married four times. Besides Eissen, there were six other children from the marriages. Izzy proclaimed that Howard had an exceptional bedside manner. Just when Clara would begin developing a closeness with a wife she became an ex-wife. She finally gave up in that department. At each wedding, Clara would declare that Howard was strictly

Izzy's friend. It was also noteworthy that Howard was part of the breakfast club.

EIGHT

Diversions come in various forms and, unfortunately, many come at the least welcome times. After rereading the book, Izzy had a nagging incentive to write more. Yet, a series of activities involving the grandchildren drew him away from the creative mode as well as away from the house. As is evident for all who go through it, the best part of grandchildren is not the grandchildren themselves but your own children. You get to see them gain a new appreciation of what is involved in parenting. They get to know first-hand what their parents had to go through with them. Another prime example showing in some respects that life is backwards. Energy is also wasted on the young. Just when you get to the stage in life where you have figured out how best to use energy and how to maximize results, the energy has waned.

It was a bit of a startling revelation when Gladys, the youngest granddaughter, said to him that he was the oldest person she knew. When he asked her how many old people she did know, she had to take a moment before responding that he was the only one she could think of. Young people should be exposed to many old folks and more often the better. Of course, it needs to work the other way around, too. Not enough elderly persons are closely involved with youngsters. That is why he thought it was a good idea when he read about a new planned community that had a child day care in the front of a building with a retirement facility behind that. A natural intermingling was inevitable. There were even extra benches around the perimeter of the playground.

The elderly can and should impart to the young the wisdom that experience has revealed to them. As the review of past events with Cheron, Jacob, and Francine made it clear, Izzy had learned the important lesson that it may be the worst thing to do to proceed with action on the initial inclination. Before a decision is made the different scenarios should be reflected upon and a pro and con analysis undertaken. The same process might be best for simple situations such as a choice of parking places to more serious matters where failure, loss, and disappointment are involved in your life or the lives of the ones you care about. He had also learned that many a time it is better to put what needs to be said in writing rather than just saying it. A writing can be modified before delivered. The spoken word cannot be taken back.

A philosophizing where one can rarely predict what an old man will do or not do. A great debate might be centered on which is worse – the mishaps of the elderly or the misguided deeds of the young. Now he knew why random thoughts are random. Some might argue further that random thoughts are worthless. He would not subscribe to that. It is nice to have an orderly mind, but that has little value as far as he was concerned. Content and substance are the goals, no matter the consistency. The matching other half to random thoughts is rambling utterances. As is quite evident he was real good at that.

At least the diversions did not detract from the random thoughts and rambling utterances. The basic problem with this, however, is that while they have value to him such may be completely meaningless or even inane to others. Yet, he was not living his life for others. His life was his own and he did not expect or want others to dispute that. If they did, that was their problem.

Alone with his thoughts, interspersed with the goings on around him, it was crucial for his well being to know that being alone with his thoughts was basically quite satisfying and comforting. He did not have to argue with anyone, and he did not have to make the effort to convince someone else that he was right or reasonable. While he was his most severe critic, at the same time he was his closest ally. A gray voyager is on two journeys. The outer excursion the world notes along with the aging signs. The inner journey is shielded from the world. It is entirely personal and is by far the more important trek. It defines and completes the story of the past, the present, and the future.

NINE

A few days later, he had the solitude once again to delve into the arena of memories. Reference to the good old days means nothing to the youth of today. They would balk at the slow movement of human events and reactions and would be totally frustrated in having to make their own fun. Too bad they will never get a taste of that kind of life. It sure would be good for them, and he dared to say that some might even prefer it.

He had almost forgotten a weekly ritual that did not sound like much in the telling but sure was enjoyable in the living. The Blue laws were in effect back then so most businesses were closed on Sundays. His father loved jelly doughnuts and looked forward to having them for breakfast on Sunday, his only day off. The bakery closed at 5:00 each day, so at 4:45 on Saturday Izzy would go there and Janice would have saved him six of those baked items. There was just enough time for her to clutch him to her monster breasts and for him to give her the fifty cents for the delightful morsels. The sweet aroma permeated through the bag as he carried it home, and he was tempted more than once to partake of the feast. It would have been easy enough to proclaim that only five had been available. Yet, the good old days also had a basic premise of honesty in every day living. He also never was good at lying, not really seeing any benefit in it. How could you possibly fully enjoy something that you had to lie about? Conscience coming to the fore, another scarce commodity in modern society. He often thought about those who served and died in the wars to protect the values of our nation and how they would roll over in their graves if they knew the values they died for were diminished and in a state of great disrepair. Those values tarnished and obscured by home grown terrorism, school and other mass shootings, senseless crime, drugs, hate crimes, road rage, willful killing of police officers, sex trafficking, and a host of other despicable entries in the journal of life. Sure, there were criminals and some bad people back then, but the basic faith in the goodness of society and people was preeminent. Anyway, he loved his father and took special happiness in watching him digest two of the doughnuts before giving one to each of the other family members. That was a special warm memory. A simple pleasure in an uncomplicated time. It almost sounded like a book title.

Faces and names from long ago filtered through his mind. Why he should recall some and not all was a mental mystery, and it became a sort of game to remember someone and then to try and affix a sound reason for the recall.

In high school, students were seated at desks in alphabetical order. His desk was always behind Doris Demonico. She was a high spirited Italian girl with long black hair. She was very smart, and was constantly raising her hand to recite an answer or to ask a question. Izzy's often reaction was *Why didn't I think of that?* Doris never seemed to wear the same outfit of clothes more than once, at least as far as he could tell. He figured the family had money and it was easy for her to have an extensive wardrobe. In all of those years she hardly ever spoke to him, and in hindsight he assumed she thought he was too stupid or boring to be bothered with. To placate himself a bit he supposed she might have been just pretending he was no one to be reckoned with. He liked to think that her intelligence led her to great success in life, maybe as one of the first female corporate executives or among the first women to be elected to public office. When he did a search on Google he found nothing about her but she may have done great things under a married name before the computer age. He once had a female student that reminded him of her. That student became a full partner at a Wall Street law firm shortly in her career. Of course, maybe the potential never materialized and Doris settled for a life without notoriety and fanfare. In the absence of knowing, Izzy liked to think she made it big time.

His closest friend in Brooklyn in elementary school was Saul Racine. He was a bit chubby, and could make his belly shake at will. Izzy could not do that, so he liked to say that Saul had a special talent. Saul lived a block away, and they walked together to and from school, often joined by others who happened to tag along. By far, their favorite activity was to take the trolley down Ocean Avenue to Coney Island. That was to a youngster a truly magical place. All sorts of amusement rides could be found there, as well as games stretched along the length of the boardwalk. The crowds were festive, and laughter filled the air. Over the years, they played every game and rode each ride multiple times. The only one they did not go on was the Parachute Jump. You had to be twenty-one to go on it, and it was truly intimidating as it reached up to the sky. Their favorite place was the Steeplechase where you could enter for one price and go on as many rides and as often as you wanted to. It was probably the precursor for the Disney theme parks. Of course, they always stopped at Nathan's for one of their legendary foot long hot dogs. Nathan's was a whole square block big, and you could go to the counter on any of the four sides. Izzy could almost taste one now as he closed his eyes and imagined his choppers sinking into one of those delights oozing with sauerkraut and mustard. Nathan's is still there and so are a bunch of rides although on a smaller scale. High rise development has taken over much of the area. The Parachute Jump and the Steeplechase have long since been gone.

Saul's' father was a night watchman, and he wound up getting a job in Queens so the family moved there where they had some relatives living there as well. Even a close friendship for youngsters is jeopardized by time and space. One time Izzy Googled Saul's name with no apparent success as to where he was and what had become of him. Belly shaking is not the kind of distinction for a computer entry. As with other things in his past, the reality is gone as the memory lives on.

TEN

As Izzy walked across the University grounds towards the Library for his weekly volunteer assignment, he took special notice of the ramps at the entrance to each building making each wheelchair accessible. Such were part of the fruits of his endeavors, and it was truly satisfying to make note of it. It also led him to think of Cheron. Meeting and knowing her was a life changing event for him, a turning point. Leaving the romantic repercussions aside, it had led Izzy to a rewarding life long career as a champion for the disabled. A turning point for other people may not be as clear cut. In fact, for Aaron in the book he was writing he had not yet conceived of a turning point. A first reaction might be his relationship with Renee. Yet, it did not really have an impact on his life. He knew he had to be patient, and an idea would come to him perhaps when he least expected it. Of course, not every life has a major turning point. There could be a series of minor turning points, maybe even barely noticeable.

Perhaps, Aaron might be a vehicle to explore a concept that Izzy had wrestled with. Is a turning point only when it arises naturally, that is with stimulus of others or as a result of an important event? Or could one create a turning point? If one wants to change direction in life, can a turning point be conceived to ease the way? Or, is it just an excuse to justify change? Can one really call it a turning point when it does not lead to a change without intention?

Thinking in terms of turning points did make looking back clearer and more productive. Izzy discussed this at length with Brian so that he might see where he was in life now that the divorce was final. Brian was also a pervasive and deliberate person. He had already concluded that he had never loved Shelly. He had deluded himself into thinking that the weaknesses she had would be overcome by his steady presence. It was a poor basis for a marriage and a life in common. He now owed it to himself to find a true love. This was his turning point.

Izzy started to think that maybe he was over analyzing everything. Perhaps, there was a natural element in fate and that one might benefit just by seeing where the random winds might take the hot air balloon. Yet, that is difficult to do for a thinker. Reasons, options, and alternatives crop up to block the supposedly natural order of things. Then there is the factor of control. A thinker has control of his life to some degree, even if he deludes himself into believing that. It happens because his thoughts lead to a plan for it to happen that way. The problem with all of that, of course, is that one does not know what may happen or even what one may want to happen. Thinking is a two-edged sword. It can cut through ambiguity or it can slice a whole sequence into tiny pieces so that the total picture is lost. As is obvious, one can think too much or too little. And, if one thinks about balance or a reasonable compromise position, the best possible thought can be lost.

ELEVEN

There were a number of early morning thought fests on the office sofa where he would revisit such an outlook. In the absence of an actual new turning point in his life, should or could he invent a new one? Where would it lead him? The idea then came to him to first try it with Aaron, the main character in the book he was writing. Not only would he test his ability to create one, it would serve as a vehicle for judging its reasonableness and effectiveness. Most of the pros and cons might surface along the way.

Aaron knew for his own survival that something had to change in his life. His doctor had tried different medicines to treat the depression. Each seemed to work for awhile, but after a short period he would slip back into the old pattern of inertia causing frustration and despair. Each retrogression brought him to an even lower spot than previous setbacks.

He had been a rational man most of his life, and he should be able to exercise enough reason on his own to help himself. There was no denying that he had all of the ingredients for a contented life. There was a caring and devoted wife. Their two daughters had never been in any trouble and had gone on to happy and fulfilling lives. There were no financial difficulties in his retirement. He had friends and an assortment of activities to challenge his mind and occupy the time. Their dearest friends were Jerry and Helen Winters. Besides sharing special occasions, they played bridge nearly every Friday night for over thirty years, alternating at their respective homes. So, why was he not happy, or at least at a point of sustained satisfaction? Why was he despondent and restless? If self analysis is at times accurate or at least marginally reasonable, the conclusion he came to was that there was one vital ingredient missing in his life. The closest he could put it into words was that he never had an adventure. There had never been an upheaval or a totally unplanned or unexpected event involving danger or risk to his physical, mental, or emotional condition that had forced him to depend solely on himself to understand and benefit from such an occurrence. He was not referring to some overt action such as committing a crime. It was not anything like a story book adventure such as sailing a boat across the ocean or climbing Mt. Everest or going on a safari in Africa. It had to be something personal to and for him, perhaps even something that only he could sense or feel.

So, what could be done in the absence of an actual adventure? At his age, the chances were remote that a genuine adventure would come along, or if it did there was a distinct likelihood he might not recognize it. Could or should he invent one? If so, how does one go about doing that? After mulling it over, he decided it might be helpful to make a list of possibilities.

1. Learn to ride a motorcycle; buy one; and then join a
        motorcycle club.

2. Since he had equated in all of his deliberations about his
        life that an old voyager views the terrain of his
        existence from a hot air balloon, he should take up
        that enterprise.

3. After researching opportunities, open a business.

4.   Find an unusual love interest.

He dwelled on each item for several days and was unable to think of any additions to the list. So, he isolated each one and analyzed it as best he could. He did not have to think long and hard about motorcycles. That would surely be an adventure but also a hardship and too dangerous for a man of his age with poor eyesight and slow reflexes. Practical measures would certainly emerge, such as getting insurance at his age and condition. Also, how could he find and join a motorcycle club without a Bahama Mamma?

A hot air balloon, while having special significance, would once again seem to demand a more youthful prerequisite, not to mention what might be a prohibitive expense. It would probably also have numerous practical negatives.

Opening a business was an intriguing idea, but once again because of his age he would not have the stamina for retail hours, not to mention the endurance and patience to carry planning into action and affording adequate time for development. Besides, it might be all consuming and he was certain he would not have the temperament and stability to enjoy it.

Of the four options, obtaining a love interest appeared to be the most feasible at first blush. Yet, it would probably be the least achievable because it did not all depend on him. What woman would be interested in an old mentally and emotionally weak man? He was no longer physically attractive, if he ever was, and unable to perform sexually. So, in effect, what would a love interest really do for him?

Izzy had to force himself to stop writing. He had been totally absorbed by Aaron's deliberations, and for a brief moment he sensed there were two of him. An author gives life to the character, but can the character also give a form of life to the author?

TWELVE

The major problem with memories, particularly if analysis is part of the scene, is that it raises the level of frustration. A keen desire to relive the event ushers forth a wish to be transported back in time with full participation under the tempting influence of hindsight. Of course, this is all accompanied by the oft-stated reference *If I only knew then what I know now*. Would or could it make a difference?

He would not be able to explain it, but a saying came to mind that he had run across many years ago. *When you find out you can make mistakes you know you are onto something*. If he had made a mistake it was because he had taken a chance. Mistakes can and should be a means of learning, especially if a similar situation arises again. Some do not learn by mistakes. Of course, a monumental accomplishment is garnered when one can learn from the mistakes made by others. Assuming one knows all of the facts and circumstances, it is not always clear that the best course of action had been taken. Whether that rises to the level of a mistake depends on the consequences. A personal outlook and agenda enter into the decision-making.

As he looked back in time, he had made what might best be described as numerous minor mistakes. A major mistake undoubtedly ripens into a regret, and as he zeroed in on events of his past he could rightfully declare that he had few regrets about what he did or did not do. The one haunting regret was about

Cheron. Nothing could change that. Looking ahead, would it be a mistake to seek out a new turning point? If so, would he regret doing it? Or, conversely, might it be a mistake not to shift to a new road? Could such inaction become a regret?

Perhaps, he was getting too bogged down in theories rather than plotting actions. Yet, that was an inherent part of being a lawyer with the addition of a growing procrastination as well as dwindling patience and tolerance, all attributed to the doubts of an old voyager. He would rationalize by saying that doubts are better than misgivings, but that might not be true. Even if true, not always true.

He needed a break. He found Clara in the kitchen and suggested that they take the dogs for a walk. She was usually up to that believing it was good exercise for all of them.

Izzy took a deep breath as they walked along. He tried to look at everything they passed carefully, and to his surprise he noted things that had not registered with him before. Even some of the people he had seen numerous times he observed features that were bypassed earlier. There was a distinct lesson here. He needed to take the same careful approach in examining the past and the future.

Back at the house, he took a nap. He was not sure if it was the walk or the mental exercise that had tired him out. One thing for sure was that he tired more easily these days. Despite the concept, he was sure there was no way to grow old gracefully. The best one could do would be to keep resistance within reasonable limits, whatever that might be.

THIRTEEN

A truism often discounted is that time and events can at times right a problem or produce a solution. There was no way he could know in advance when he went to the University for his Library stint that this would be the day that his life would take that elusive new turn.

Because of his professional background as well as his early involvement with Cheron, he had a tendency to focus on people in wheelchairs, especially women. When he entered the main reading room to sign in and request his assignment for the day, at one of the tables was a young woman and the wheelchair she was in was set by the table as she read the book before her. He had not seen her before. As he approached the service desk, the woman glanced up and smiled at him. It was a warm and beguiling smile, and the dimples in her cheeks made her appear younger than she probably was.

After he received the assignment, he approached the woman. His Library whisper was well versed. "You gladdened the heart of an ole buzzard when you smiled at him."

Her voice was mellow and diction cultured and he assumed she was a student. "I didn't see an old buzzard. All I saw was a man with kind eyes." Another tantalizing smile. "Besides I know who you are."

"You do?"

"I dare say there is not a disabled person alive who does not know our champion." Yet another endearing smile. "I have been waiting for you. They said you would be in today."

"An anticipated arrival is as good as it gets."

"You are also more handsome than your pictures and the times I saw the televised hearings."

It was his turn to smile. "Kind remarks to match my eyes."

"I have always considered a full head of gray hair a mark of distinction and highly distinguished. It is the snow cap atop the mountain of the person. And you are a mountain among men."

He noticed the intent stare from the librarian at the front desk. "Let's go to the snack area in the lobby to talk some more. We may be disturbing others here."

She left the book open on the table, a sure sign she intended to return after the talk. He pushed the wheelchair to the lobby. Since it was early, there were only a few people around. "Would you like a cup of coffee?," he offered.

"No, thanks, but you go ahead."

"I have already had my quota for the day." He sat on the bench alongside where he had stopped the wheelchair. "You know who I am. Have I met you before?

The warm smile reappeared. "No, we have not met before. I am Tessa, although everyone calls me just Tess. Tessa Richmore Caulfield is my full name. I am a Professor of English here at the University."

"I was about to castigate myself if I had met you before that I did not remember such a momentous occasion."

"Have you always been such a sweet talker?"

"No, not really. I do feel inspired at the moment."

"Are you curious about why I was waiting for you?"

"I figured you would get around to telling me. Do I owe you money?"

Her laugh was genuine. "No, but that is an idea."

"Cancel that idea," he retorted.

"I won't keep you in suspense any longer, Mr. Denton."

"Izzy, please," he interrupted her.

"Alright, Izzy. I teach an advanced creative writing class. I have just given them an assignment to write a story where the main character is a champion of a cause. I cannot think of a greater champion than you. I was hoping I could get you to come as a guest lecturer one day to inspire them to greatness."

"I can certainly do that, and will enjoy it I am sure. Do I get any other kind of reward?"

She hesitated before that warm smile appeared again. "Enjoyment is its own reward. But, if I think you have done well in the motivation department I will treat you to lunch afterward."

"The treat will be your company."

"There goes that sweet talk again."

"When would you like me to do this?"

"Does next Tuesday work for you?"

"Sure."

"Good. The class meets at 10:00 A.M. in room 127 of Channing Hall. Thank you, Izzy."

"No, thank you, Tess."

He wheeled her back to the Library table and went off to his assignment for the day. He did not get much of the work done. Between distractions provided by the books, images of that enchanting smile and replicas of that delightful laugh nestled in his mind. Was this Aaron's love interest?

FOURTEEN

It was as if he was before a class at the law school again. A sea of young, attentive faces confronted him. It was so quiet he could hear his own labored breathing.

After that glowing introduction by Professor Caulfield, I would like to give you a glimpse into not so much a secret as an exciting fact of our existence. A truly satisfying life, in the sense of accomplishment, is not how far you go or how high you climb. It is what you do for others. When I speak of others, that does not necessarily mean other people. Animals, the environment, government, and organizations, can be considered, just to name some.

When I was your age, if I can clearly remember back that far, I had no idea what I wanted to do with my life. I dare say at that point I did not even know who I was, where I wanted to be, and where I wanted to go or even could go. I guess in today's world you would call that an identity crisis. One event and one experience changed all that. And that may be all it takes. And it is not just that kind of happening that is crucial. One has to be receptive to it and willing to explore and investigate all of the nuances. In one of my college classes there was a girl in a wheelchair. I had seen people in wheelchairs, persons with disabilities before, without giving it much thought. It had not registered in my mind that they were actual people with all of the same hopes and dreams except that they had to tolerate the stigma attached to their condition as well as overcome the physical and emotional obstacles that society thrust on them. This girl opened my eyes and my heart to the plight of such individuals. She recited part of a poem to me that I committed to memory, and it still lingers in that rusty compartment to this day.

> Today, upon a bus, I saw a lovely girl
> > with golden hair;
> I envied her, she seemed so gay,
> > and wished I were as fair
> When suddenly she rose to leave,
> I saw her hobble down the aisle;
> She had one leg, and wore a crutch,
> > and as she passed – a smile.
> O God, forgive me when I whine.
> I have two legs. The world is mine.

Verses follow pertaining to those who are blind and deaf. We need to be appreciative of what we have and be aware of and assist those less fortunate. A helping hand or even just a kind word will not only make them feel significant it will also make you feel good.

Anyway, as they say, the rest is history. I like to think I filled a necessary niche. That I may have been successful I do not attribute to my intellect or any special talent, the need was there. The cause demanded action. If I had not come along, eventually another would have picked up the banner and carried it into battle. We are all heroes in our heart, mind, and soul. It just takes a combination of factors to bring out that part of our being. I have bored you long enough. If there are any questions, fire away.

It seemed as if every student had raised a hand. The questions were varied and pointed, so it was evident they had enjoyed the talk. The now famous entrancing smile from Tess indicated she had prided herself on the choice of guest speaker.

After the class period, Izzy approached Tess. "Well, how did I do?"

"You did just as I knew you would."

"Do I get a quiet lunch with you?"

"As quiet as the cafeteria will allow. My driver does not come until late in the day."

"My car will hold your chair if you have time for us to go elsewhere."

"My next class is at three. It is your reward, so your choice."

He wheeled her to his car in the parking lot. When he lifted her out of the chair, she was nearly weightless. It reminded him of the times he had done the same for Cheron. It flashed through his mind that this might be a form of a second chance, a second chance to capture what he once had lost.

They ate at a small Italian cafe about a mile from the University. They dined on the back patio and there were no other patrons there.

Besides being introduced to a quick wit and a discerning intellect, he learned much about her past. She was relaxed with him and opened up more than she was accustomed to. One of the traits he learned in his youth that had worked well for him his entire life was that he was a good listener. It was also a delight to listen to her. Speaking brought a fetching beauty to her face that was not apparent otherwise. Too bad most people do not allow inner beauty to be perceived on the outside.

Tessa Richmore Caulfield had deformed legs due to a birth

mishap in the uterus. Her parents were poor but hard working. They could only give her minimum assistance and guidance for a situation overwhelming to them. In those days society was an adversary and not receptive to a body that could not fend for itself. Other children called her a freak. There were many more tears than laughs. A probing intellect accompanied by a fierce determination led her to overcome, or at least accept and make the best of, many obstacles. The fruits of Izzy's successes gave her the right and accessibility to many of the things she might have been denied. A love for reading and writing made it easy for her to get a full academic scholarship to college. She became a success story in her own way.

Echoing Cheron's experience of being deprived and denied many of the normal aspects of a young life, she readily admitted with great remorse that many of the normal actions and activities of her contemporaries were absent for her. She had never dated and had never had any boy show a romantic interest in her. She always felt she had much love to give because her heart was full and it was depressing being thwarted. A high intellect brings a necessary resignation, although there is the nagging feeling of missing out on a beautiful part of a complete life.

Izzy listened intently, the admissions not new or surprising. Life can be difficult at best, and it becomes even harder when greater effort is needed to accept the burdens. It was a natural action for him when he extended his hand and covered her dainty hand with his. Empathy is a great motivator. As he listened, it became obvious to him that she was the one who needed a love interest. The reality became even clearer to him that such a love interest was not an ill-conceived romantic overture from an old, worn out man. As much as he might wish it otherwise, a gray voyager is not a super hero. A gray voyager is also certainly no

Rudolph Valentino, another image revealing his antiquarianism.

FIFTEEN

No question about it, a gray voyager is not a superhero or a classic heart throb, and is further bogged down by a long life of sobering experiences which lead to decisions and actions based on tempered inward deliberations and careful actions. Tess needed a love interest more than he did. In fact, even if the most delightful dream bubble might burst right before his eyes he really did not need a love interest. This was a form of shock to his emotional composite. Perhaps, in his writer's mind he had just been enamored with the idea. After a long personal sigh, he decided he would put off any further deliberations and analysis of this major development to his psyche until a protracted period of solitude would do it justice.

Izzy sorted out in his mind some of his former students who might be a match for Tess. There was no settling on a viable possibility. Tess might be his daughter the way he cross examined potential candidates in his mind. That family image kept bringing his thought processes to a most logical choice – his son, Brian.

Brian's divorce was now final. Izzy had imbued an attentive and caring attitude for the disabled throughout Brian's growing years, not only from the recitation of his career and beliefs but also as part of the nurturing process for a future empathetic adult. He had not thought at the time that Shelly was a good life partner for Brian, but he just hoped it would work out for the best. Clara also had some misgivings, although her staunch optimistic belief in family overshadowed objections. The grandchildren then became the focus as the years filtered by.

Even as a child Brian had a fascination for maps, especially treasure maps. A family trip to Prince Edward Island in Canada and the boy's coveted souvenir was a map of all of the sunken vessels off the coast. So, it was no surprise when he became a cartographer. Izzy doubted there was enough money in that to support a family, yet surprisingly he did well at it. Too bad he could not draw a map for his own happy future. Izzy would change that be arranging a meeting with Tess.

Izzy might have to reconsider his old age accomplishments. Without being aware of it at any prior time, maybe he was meant to be a matchmaker. A report on the first date between Tess and Brian was, by every account, a glowing success. It is a glorious feat to make a person happy. Added exuberance follows when two people are led to elation.

Of course, this did not solve his personal quandery. He still felt in many ways neither here nor there. Something was missing from his life, and if it was not a particular love interest then it was an elusive commodity that added to his trepidation. As best he might describe it, he had a restless spirit. That was probably one of the last things an old man would want to wrestle with. Yet, what he wanted to do and needed to do was, as usual, two different things.

SIXTEEN

A form of lethargy took hold as the days slipped by. Only routine disguised his inner anguish, and it was apparent that he had to take control of the hot air balloon symbolizing his life. Working on the book might be an answer, but he was not steady of hand or mind to grapple with Aaron's turmoil as well as his own.

A saying he had come across some time ago came to mind. *There is no beginning; there is no end. There is only the passion of life.* So, what or where was his passion? As exemplified by his career path and family he had much passion for others. He now firmly believed that a person owes a passion for himself. In high school he knew a beautiful young girl who completely shunned dating and the social activities the other girls were absorbed in. She played the cello beautifully and that was her passion. It displaced nearly every other facet of life. It was her ultimate satisfaction. Was the writing of the book to be his passion? Yet, it did not consume him, and there were many moments he did not even think about it. There was no compulsion to write during waking hours, and rarely did he dream about it. There was no burning quest to finish it.

One additional problem with memories is that the emphasis is on the pleasure of the hindsight as distinguished from the emotions at the earlier time. Perhaps, it was a wrong approach to have reviewed his life before proceeding on with it. Maybe, it would have been better to just pretend this was a new starting place and he had to find a way to get to the next stepping stone.

While he probably should have been prepared for any shock to his reverie, any event to topple the apple cart, he was not in any way set to face the event that took place while he was deep in thought. Clara had gone with three friends to a matinee at a dinner theater some thirty miles away. One of the other ladies was driving and Clara was in the back seat. It was raining and the driver lost control of the car on a curve and skidded off the highway with the vehicle side forcefully striking a tree. All four women were deemed to have been killed instantly. That Clara had not suffered was probably the only relieving thought. The incident wiped his mind of everything and anything else.

Izzy had revised their wills when all of the children reached adulthood. Clara's will left everything to Izzy. At that time they had decided on cremation as the most reasonable choice upon death. The ashes were now contained in a plain walnut box that Izzy set on the mantle until he would decide what to do with them.

At the memorial service tears flowed and sobs rippled through the crowd. The cruel tragedy accentuated the helpless and hopeless feelings. The large gathering included all of the family and friends, as well as the breakfast club. Tess was there even though Clara had not yet met her. All of the children and two of the eldest grandchildren spoke about the woman they loved and of the warm family times. Izzy was the last to speak, his voice raspy and hesitant. The ramblings were long and painful, and just when he thought he was finished a new thought needed to be expressed. To capture the essence of the life of one loved is no easy task. Long after the service he would denounce himself for leaving something out.

He used the dogs as an excuse to be alone that night. The dogs kept looking for Clara, and there was no way for him to explain to them that she would no longer be there. He could barely understand it himself.

He half expected to have a feeling of guilt for his premise of possibly finding an outside love interest, although he did not since he had abandoned that notion when he matched Tess with Brian. There was just an ever increasing regret that he had not embraced her that morning before she left and to tell her that he loved her. One should always do that since the moments ahead are truly unknown. Many of the memories of their togetherness edged into his thoughts as he tried to sleep. He was exhausted but his mind would not let him rest. Mental peace only comes at a high personal price, if at all.

The memories faded in and out, especially of the times he and Clara had shared a laugh or a special feeling. When they went out shortly after marrying to buy their first new car, Izzy suggested to Clara that she pull out some of their old clothing and doctor them up further to look quite faded and threadbare. They might get a better deal if they presented the impression they were poor and struggling. It was as if it was a costume party event. It was not certain that it produced the result intended. However, after they left the dealership they found a Chinese restaurant they had not been to before. The owner took one look at their clothing and insisted they pay for the meal before being served.

SEVENTEEN

Jenny and Nadine, the grief-stricken daughters, did not want him to be alone. They suggested he sell the house and live with either of them. Both had large homes and offered that his privacy would be respected. As diplomatically as he could phrase it, he responded that there was no way he would give up an independent life until and unless he was no longer able to fend for himself. To assure them, he had both Howard and Eissen telephone them to state that Izzy was physically fit to be on his own.

Physically, he was truly on his own. He hired a cleaning service for a weekly effort on the house. The dogs were in an easy and manageable maintenance schedule. His eating habits were not difficult or demanding, and the daughters often dropped off meals for him. He continued with his volunteering for delivery of meals for the senior center and tasks at the Library. The breakfast club still met regularly, although there seemed to be less joviality.

Emotionally, it was another story. Adjusting to the absence of what had been a pervasive force in his life was difficult. Clara's presence surrounded his every movement. The furniture, knickknacks, and family pictures on the walls and in frames on much of the furniture were constant reminders of a woman who had been so much a part of his being. The marital bed was cold and lonely.

Early one morning as he was drinking coffee on the sofa in the office with the dogs curled up against him, he finally figured it out. He was not sure if he was relieved or in the throes of a new and perhaps even greater anguish. The book was his passion after all. Not all passion is earthshaking, obvious, or heated. Maybe the subdued passions are equally as vital.

Once the revelation sank in, all the pieces came together. His life was not empty. A new adventure was not needed. It was Aaron's plight, Aaron's dilemma. While a search and review of early memories was a tantalizing mental exercise, it was in fact an exploration of Aaron's personality and possible future development. Now it made sense that he would ponder at times where his real self left off and the fictionalized character began. It was up to Aaron to straighten out his life, to satisfy his own wants and needs, and to move in a new direction. Having a fictionalized alter ego is an escape hatch.

So, despite not having alluring qualities, Aaron decided to find and nurture a love interest. It would be tempting to initiate a relationship online, and since there were many such avenues it would be the easiest way to go. Yet, he was old fashioned, and it would be more meaningful if it occurred in person and an accidental or on purpose meeting.

He went to the large shopping mall nearby. He sat on a bench and studied the women that walked by. All ages and sizes meandered by, not a single one noticing him. That was not

good for his plan or his ego. Then he tried the supermarket. Many women were there as he wandered down the aisles. Again, there was no connection, either obvious or subtle.

He went to the public library and surveyed the posted listing

*of book clubs. He jotted down a few of the telephone numbers
and email addresses. In theory this might be a good source
for meeting someone but he was not optimistic about it. He
was not a great reader, and his intellect was limited. At the
very least, he was aware of his shortcomings.*

*Just as he was about to leave the library, he noticed the
librarian sitting behind the book checkout counter. She was
staring at him. She was pleasant looking, and probably
younger than the full head of gray hair might indicate. He
smiled, and she smiled in return. As he approached the counter
he studied her features. A short, stubby nose barely held up
her glasses with wide brown eyes behind them, full lips, and a
pale complexion. It was only when he reached the counter
did he realize she was sitting in a wheelchair.*

Izzy halted his writing with a jerk to his body. He had
no idea before he wrote it that the woman was going to be in a
wheelchair. Was the lingering influence of Cheron so pervasive
that it guided his mind to his hand? Or, was it merely a reaction to
the more recent meeting with Tess?

A draining weariness came over him, undoubtedly as a
result of all that he had been through. He left the office and sat
on the porch with the dogs close by. His world had changed, and
maybe he was too old to adapt to it. Uncertainty is difficult to
handle at any age, but it seems worse for the elderly. It is not the
sort of feeling one wants by the exit door from life.

EIGHTEEN

It was several days before he could get back to writing, although he thought about Aaron's situation often. He played around with different scenarios in his mind, not sure which was best or even manageable. If Aaron's love interest was to materialize, it had to be handled just right.

Aaron was not sure what he could or should say. It mattered not as the words came out in a hushed whisper so none of the library patrons might hear. "Is my book overdue?" The touch of humor was a surprise to him.

Her smile was tantalizing. "You are overdue."

"Better late than never."

"You don't remember me, do you?"

He studied the features and glanced at the wheelchair. "No, but shame on me."

"I get a break in fifteen minutes and we can go to the lobby to talk. I'll tell you then if you haven't remembered it all."

The minutes dragged by, and Aaron could not believe he could not remember meeting such an attractive woman. His mind was blank. He found this significant. More often than not these days his physical, mental, and emotional prowess failed him rather than something he could depend on.

He followed her to the lobby when she wheeled herself out after another librarian relieved her. There was a certain grace in her movement, and for an instant he was baffled by it.

Her look was steady and she grinned knowingly. "Still no recollection?"

"Sadly, no."

"Maybe this will help. My name is Sally Plough."

His silence was an obvious admission of his stupidity. Then he uttered weakly, "I am more disappointed in myself than you are in me."

"I am just amused by it. You will laugh when I tell you. You haven't changed much, so I recognized you right away. I, on the other hand, am quite different. I was not in a wheelchair back then. I was the high school teacher for each of your children, and we also served on the PTA together."

"Oh, of course. Forgive me, please. What happened?"

"My legs were all but destroyed in a car accident, the same accident that killed my husband. It was seven years ago, although it seems like an eternity."

He put his hand on her sweatered arm. "I am so sorry."

"I am living with my daughter,
and I sense I am an imposition. She has a small house
and two children. Her husband does not approve, and has
often suggested I get my own place and hire whatever help
I need."

"Stressful, I am sure. Do you work here?"

"No. I just volunteer two days a week to give my daughter
time alone."

"I am retired and, frankly, I have difficulty filling up my time."

Her voice was mesmerizing. He surmised she had been a
good teacher. "You might consider volunteering too, maybe
at a library, hospital, senior center, or a host of other places
that can use extra help."

"I would like to volunteer spending some time with you."

Her modesty pleased him. "That would not be very rewarding.
I cannot do much and very dependent on others."

"I can handle it."

Izzy had to put the writing aside when the telephone rang. It was Nadine checking on him. By the time he chatted with her for awhile he was not in the mood to get back to the writing.

He took the dogs for a walk, and his mind was immersed

in conflicting thoughts. He was not sure of the direction that Aaron's new adventure would take. In fact, he was not sure if a love interest was the main device. Perhaps, it was the notion that another person can be such a strong influence as to alter a life pattern and expectation. He would have to resolve this before proceeding.

NINETEEN

The dawn was still a good hour away. He already drank a pot of coffee and was ensconced on the sofa in his office with the dogs. His mood was pensive. At one point he was sure he heard Clara stirring in another part of the house, and the sadness settled heavily in his heart.

The two most troubling aspects of old age that he had encountered so far were a loss of the taste of food and a growing lack of patience. The fading ability to fully taste food was, according to Howard, the direct result of an impaired sense of smell. Izzy thought it might have been all the Chinese food he had over the years. As for a quick and burgeoning impatience, it was most troubling in contrast to the calm demeanor and great patience he had as a younger man. Now, his frustration arose at even the slightest actions he deemed stupid or unnecessary, and he was troubled by any inane behavior. The peaceful moments a gray voyager should nestle in were dwindling away, and his agitation made him disgruntled. Clara's calming effect had even been taken from him.

Izzy liked to think that his mind was perfectly intact. He had already reviewed the turning points in his life. Now, as his wakeful moment produced a certain clarity that he could only describe as a revealing moment, he searched his memory for similar occurrences in his past. It was certainly a revealing moment when he decided he would become a defender and protector of the legal rights of the disabled. It was a revealing moment when he came to the conclusion that Clara was to be his life partner even overshadowing the sense that Cheron had been the love of his life. Most recently, it was eye-opening to confirm that Brian was a better match for Tess than he was.

Now, a crucial and most surprising revelation came as a bolt of lightning in the personal storm he was trying to survive in. Aaron, in the final analysis, was not his alter ego. All along there had only been Izzy. And, he did not need a story to make his way. He did not need to write the book as any mental or emotional release. Whatever the future might hold for him, he need not vent it in his imagination. He had to live it. He had to do that without distractions and sidetracks. A personal honesty within and without surely is a revelation. He recalled the powerful lines from a poem by William Ernest Henley:

> It matters not how strait the gate,
>> How charged with punishments the scroll,
> I am the master of my fate:
>> I am the captain of my soul.

He gathered all the notes and writings on the book and put them in the filing cabinet. Then he archived the computer files. Actually, he felt satisfied with this decision, knowing full well at any future time all would not be lost if there was a reversal of his mind set. There was now a relief from the pressure of having to write. Grief can change passions.

Little did he know at the time that an even greater revelation lay ahead. It came when he stared at a print of a duck that hung on the wall in his office. He had a certain fascination with ducks since he was a boy and had seen a mallard for the first time. Not a city person's typical reaction. On the bottom of the print just above the frame were the words *From the Biltmore House Library*. It was the picture that he and Clara had bought at the gift shop at the Biltmore House in Asheville, North Carolina on their first visit there nearly thirty years ago. The mansion and grounds held a special allure for city folk, and its historical significance of another time and society was captivating. They had gone there several times since then, and were particularly enthralled when they went at Christmas time when each of the rooms in the mansion were decorated as an early Christmas would have been. It was truly another world, and of all of the scant places they had gone to it was Clara's favorite. It would be there that he would scatter Clara's ashes.

That decision eased the way to the next step his mind was racing towards, a decision the children and even the breakfast club would not be in favor of. He was going to move to Asheville and volunteer at the Biltmore House.

Jenny and Nadine were adamantly opposed to the idea, and they knew they would have no success in trying to sway him from a course that he now had his mind set on. Brian said nothing but inwardly admired his father's gumption. He knew where he had inherited his own spirit from.

Before putting the house up for sale, Izzy boxed up all of the momentoes of Clara and the family. Grouped together there were more than he thought there might be, and they told a story that repeatedly brought tears to his eyes. He had concentrated so much on the memories of his childhood that he had neglected to pay homage to the years since so filled with times of joy, satisfaction, and insights. He told the girls that they would have all of these when he passed on.

He did a computer search of houses in the Asheville area,

and with the help of a real estate agent he selected and bought a small log cabin just built in the mountains. A virtual tour of the place, its setting, and the views which matched the views from the mansion itself, satisfied him enough that he did not even have to see the place for himself before concluding it was the perfect spot. He knew the dogs would love it, especially the wrap-around porch. A large stone fireplace in the great room would have appealed to Clara.

The house sold six weeks after being put on the market. He selected only the furniture and furnishings he would want at the cabin to have the moving company pack. He let the children take anything else they might want, and the remainder was put up at auction. He traded the car in for a rugged truck, and after final good-byes to all Izzy and the dogs headed for a new life. The only question he posed to himself was, "What took me so long?"

Living in a log cabin in the mountains sure was a drastic change for a city boy. Of course, living in suburbia was somewhat of a transition. Yet, he was enthralled by the vistas and the sounds of country life. This was probably something he should have proposed to Clara years ago, as she would have been happy here as well. And, the accident would never have happened. He thought the dogs might have a problem adjusting to all the newness, but they fell right in to this new way of living and were excited with each fresh experience and smell.

The first night when he stepped out on the porch and looked up at the night sky so filled with stars not visible in city lights, he was enthralled. Clara's artistic eye would have been overwhelmed by it. The wind passing through the trees was her sigh of agreement.

TWENTY

It was easy to volunteer at the Biltmore House two mornings a week, and he was able to choose the Library as the room he would be an attendant in. The Library was very large and grand, and it suited him well. A short period of training was all he needed.

There was usually someone to talk to or to answer questions as large crowds commonly passed through the Library. It became easy to tell the first time visitors from those that had been there before. A gasp of wonder was often a tell-tale sign.

He soon found out that there was a prohibition on spreading deceased's ashes anywhere on the grounds of the mansion. He had thought that might be the case, so he had a back up plan. He planted a peach tree right behind the cabin that he could see from the back windows and spread Clara's ashes around the base of it. Peaches were Clara's favorite fruit. The tree would always be special and its harvest would be bountiful and sweet, of that he was sure.

He met his nearest neighbors a quarter of a mile down the gravel road. Lance and Denise Coorsan were middle-aged, in their second marriage, and had lived in Asheville all of their lives. Lance was a carpenter by trade, and Izzy was going to have him make a couple of bookcases because he wanted to start a duck collection to go along with the picture. Denise worked at the animal shelter, and they had a house full of rescue dogs and cats. Denise joked that they had seven four-legged children but the heart always had room for more. Denise recommended a veterinarian for his dogs.

Izzy explored all of the tourist haunts of the city, as well as many of the places Denise told him the locals liked. Just down from a large antiques mall was a series of smaller antiques shops as well as specialty stores. One of these antiques shops he found especially appealing, not only because there were a number of duck decoys for sale but the woman who owned and operated the shop was warm, friendly, and interesting to talk with. The first time he went in there were no other customers at the time so he roamed around the place unhindered. He lingered by the ducks and selected two to purchase that would look good on the bookcase Lance was to build. Then he started talking to the owner, Flora Staggart. She and her husband had started the shop some twenty years earlier soon after the mall opened as they figured there would be some good spillover traffic. They made a decent living although it was becoming more and more difficult in recent years because antiques shops were hard pressed as another casualty from the internet world. They enjoyed going to auctions and estates sales where they found most of the items to resell. There were two married children, a son living in Raleigh, North Carolina, and a daughter living in Savannah, Georgia. Flora was an avid reader, and reading was a blessing especially at slow periods in the shop. Her husband had died four years earlier from an intestinal mishap, and she continued on with the shop to fill up her days and she was comfortable with it. It was also an excuse not to have to choose which child to move close to, although grandchildren made it tempting. She visited them often, and a close friend kept the store open during her absence. Flora was intelligent and had a warm endearing personality, similar to Clara.

On his third visit to the shop, Flora invited him to go with her to one of the monthly antiques auctions she frequented. She lived only a few miles from the cabin and picked him up in her van the night of the auction. Izzy found the auction intriguing. He was surprised how many items were up for sale and wondered how all would be disposed of. Yet, the sale moved along quickly and smoothly. The auctioneer was part comic so entertaining and a master at placating and handling the bidders. Flora cautioned him not to raise his hand or make any other overt gesture during actual bidding lest he be pointed to on a particular bid. He helped Flora load the items that she won into the van.

She then took him to a late night coffee shop which made its own pastries. They lingered at the eating place for nearly two hours, and their conversation was easy and pleasant. He discovered she was twenty-three years younger than he was but that did not seem to bother her. It certainly did not matter to him.

Izzy became a regular visitor to the shop, and he would stay an hour or so and help her as she taught him about antiques. It was a fascinating world, and Izzy could readily see how some could get swept up in it.

The first time she had him for dinner, he was not at all surprised that her house was filled with antiques that had a special appeal to her and her husband. She was a very good cook, and he had the best meal he had in quite awhile.

Fall was quickly approaching, but despite the on setting chill they sat on her back porch after the meal. Both were in a reminiscent mood.

"I don't fear growing old," Flora spoke in a subdued tone. "But, I have a festering belief that there is something I need to do yet."

"I have had a similar feeling rather recently," Izzy said thoughtfully. "It can be bothersome because there are so many dead ends. I have concluded that it is perhaps better to talk oneself

Daniel Hill Zafren

77

out of such a quagmire than to get immersed in it. The way I did it was to concentrate on what I have already done and that has proven to be enough. A lifetime is short but is fuller than we usually realize. We often don't give ourselves the credit we deserve. I suppose for me, at least, coming to Asheville is my last hurrah."

"By any standard, you have accomplished much and can be proud of who you are and what you have done for others."

"I am, but when you clear a path for others to follow maybe it is just curiosity to know who they are and what they will do."

"For me, it is not so simple. I, for the lack of any other way to express it, feel I am pigeon-holed. A routine and predictable life is comforting but far from exciting. My husband was the only man I ever kissed and had sex with."

"Is that an invitation?"

"Just a statement of fact. I think often what difference it may have made in me if I had a different kind of experience when young."

"Take it from an old pro, second-guessing your life is a case of diminishing returns. You can't turn back the clock, and even if you could you would probably make the same choices all over again. As for sex, at my age snuggling and cuddling are my avenues of pleasure."

"Sounds nice, but I think you and I are destined to be close friends only. A close friend is a precious gift."

"And I will be your antiques apprentice."

"Sounds about right. I decided after my husband died that I will not marry again. Not just because he was such a good man but I do not think I could take it emotionally to lose another husband."

"I sort of feel the same way but the age factor looms larger for me than for you. Yet, we all want and need companionship, and companionship can take many forms and be in many different degrees. Companionship, after all, is the true basis for the love underlying a marriage."

"So, what you are saying is that you can be married without being married."

"Sounds too radical?"

"No, it probably makes sense. But, I will have to think about it for awhile."

TWENTY-ONE

Izzy was now submerged in the world of antiques. As he watched Flora in action and listened intently to the explanations of things both large and small, he realized there was a great deal to learn. He even looked at the antiques at the Biltmore House with a new inquisitiveness. It would have been a gratifying indulgence if he had taken an interest in antiques earlier in his life, and it probably would have been an additional activity that he and Clara could have shared, especially the hunt for the unique and potential profit makers. One profound observation that Flora had gleaned over the years was that if you have an object for sale that is missing from a collector's cache of such objects, the collector will pay dearly to have it. The true value of any antique is what one is willing to pay for it.

The week before Izzy and Flora were to take Thanksgiving trips to celebrate the holiday with their respective children, Izzy invited Flora over for a Saturday night dinner. He knew she did not open the shop on Sundays. He made what he called a super omelet because the list of ingredients that were not in it was shorter than the one of the ingredients thrown in. Flora brought an apple pie that she had made for dessert.

After the dinner and clean up, they sat on the sofa that used to be in Izzy's office and was now in front of the stone fireplace. Izzy made a fire, and they sat close together with the dogs close by their sides. The dogs had taken an instant liking to her, and she seemed to be at ease with them.

Flora reached for his hand and grasped it tightly. She spoke softly. "I am ready for you to kiss me."

He leaned towards her and gently pressed his lips against her lips that he noted trembled ever so slightly. After a few seconds he kissed her again with increased ardor. The dogs watched intently.

When the kiss was over, Flora smiled. "Are all old lawyers such good kissers?"

He smiled back. "I don't know. I never kissed one."

She laughed. "As I told you before, I never kissed another man. Just confirms I may have missed out on some momentous occasions."

After a gentle squeeze of her fingers, he whispered wistfully. "Life is far too short not to take advantage of every potential moment of pleasure that comes along. I firmly believe this."

"Without qualification?"

"Just as long as it is not hurtful or disappointing to someone close to you, yes."

"The basic problem with decisions in life is that the decision has to be made. Wouldn't it be wonderful if the decision was already made for you?"

"It would take all the fun out of it."

She kissed him fervently. "I packed an overnight bag. It is in the van. Can I be your guest for the night?"

"That decision has already been made for you."

TWENTY-TWO

As was his custom, Izzy arose before sunrise. Flora was still asleep in the bed. From the light that came from the cracked door to the bathroom, he studied her face. The similarities to Clara's features were striking, or was he just seeing into it what he wished to see? Or, was the similarity more wide-spread as the names of the two women, including demeanor, personality, and sensitivity as well?

They had held one another close most of the night, and it was the sort of pleasure that he pointed to as an opportunity not to be denied. It also had a basic human quality, an inherent powerful communication of mutual sharing and caring. In the autumn of life, or what he was now describing as the pre-winter of life, while human emotions can be more subtle they are just as powerful and endearing as one has greater control over their contours and direction.

He was certain that Clara would have wished this for him just as he would have hoped she would find solace in a new companionship for her remaining days if he had gone first. The heart is an amazing organ. Among other things, it has the capacity to enfold new and additional feelings.

He took the dogs for a walk just as the sky was brightening for a new day. It was the overall sensation of contentment that was as a fresh breeze in his mind. His thoughts were no longer cluttered with doubts, with the dilemma over the significance of memories, or the need to fix on unfinished journeys and to speculate on what might lay ahead. He, perhaps, had learned the valuable lesson that all people, particularly older folks, should clutch to their hearts and minds that since there may not be a tomorrow the present should be lived to the fullest. For a gray voyager, what lies ahead is not as important as what lies within.

Book Two

The Destination

Requiem

Under the wide and starry sky,
Dig the grave and let me lie,
Gladly did I live and gladly die,
And I laid me down with a will.

This be the verse you grave for me:
Here he lies where he longed to be;
Home is the sailor, home from sea,
And the hunter home from the hill.

— Robert Louis Stevenson

Now, Voyager, sail thou forth,
to seek and find.

— Walt Whitman

PREFACE

Assuming where one winds up is a destination, how does one know that destination is the one wanted or deserved? If there is any doubt, can there still be something beyond that? It is the kind of thought process that is unproductive because only the actual happening can resolve it. Yet, for a thinking person it is challenging. Then, of course, it might simply be a case of rationalization. For peace of mind, why not consider where you wind up as the destination that was meant to be? Of course, if the destination is not a happy or safe place, one must trudge on. Stumbling in the dark may then prove to be highly frustrating.

If the author has created the search for a destination contemplating that the search itself might prompt reconsideration of that end, the pursuit itself might actually lead to a different destination or, perhaps, a series of destinations. If, in fact, a series of destinations, the order may be crucial in the final development of the character involved in the search. All of this the author must wrestle with. And if the end is not known until it happens, will the author be contented? Will the reader be satisfied?

ONE

It was a quiet celebration for Izzy on his eighty-fifth birthday, quite unlike the festive eightieth birthday event. A person should be left alone with his thoughts on a birthday in the later years since a birthday then can be considered as a resting spot in life's travel. It is a place and time to reflect on all things, large and small. He had already spoken to all of the children and grandchildren on the telephone, graciously accepting their well wishes and noting the love in the expressed sentiments. Most of the grandchildren were now out on their own, and it took keen concentration to detail in his mind where they now were and what they were involved in. After speaking with Brian, Tess got on the line and gushed over her favorite guest lecturer. She and Brian had been married for more than three years, and there was no doubt as to their happiness. Izzy sure had that right, and was proud of his matchmaking endeavor. He almost called her Cheron but caught himself in time.

He sat on the bench he had put by the peach tree, and he could sense Clara wishing him a happy birthday. As he had predicted, the tree had repeatedly produced bountiful harvests, and he wound up giving many peaches away.

It had been a year now since Flora sold the antique shop and moved to Savannah to be with her daughter and those grandchildren. Izzy and Flora had enjoyed a close and affectionate relationship, but it was lacking any deep sense of commitment. The parting was sad but they both knew it was not earth-shaking. As a going-away present, she gave him all of the ducks from the shop, and he now had twenty-three on the shelves of the bookcases. It was an impressive collection and most visitors commented as such. He joked it took him an hour every day to feed them all, not to mention cleaning up the mess.

At different times, each of the yorkies had succumb to old age defects and he had to put them to sleep. He buried each one just beyond the peach tree. He tried to be without a dog for awhile, knowing that a dog might very well outlive him and he did not want to have the dog be alone. Denise found an older small mixed breed dog at the shelter for him and told him she would take her if things worked out that way. Interestingly, the dog's name was *Destiny*.

He had given up volunteering at the Biltmore House over a year earlier. He was still able to do it, but standing for long periods of time was increasingly uncomfortable. He told himself that he should not unnecessarily fight old age. A gradual slowdown was not a defeat as much as a battle plan.

Mentally, he was by all accounts at full tilt, and he had no reason to doubt he would stay that way until the end. Being alone with his thoughts was not depressing. The thoughtful words of Alexander Pope waffled in his mind:

> *Blest, who can unconcernedly find*
> *Hours, days, and years slide soft away*
> *In health of body, pace of mind;*
>   *Quiet by day.*

He would sit on the porch with Destiny for hours at a time staring at the mountain view, and he went wherever his thoughts took him. The hot air balloon was in free flight.

He sensed this was not the end of his journey, and in spite of a growing curiosity about what might lie ahead he was at least in this respect not impatient. Whatever it was would take its own good time in getting there. Destiny was waiting for her destiny as well.

TWO

Izzy was still in the habit of waking up early, and it often afforded the opportunity to see some spectacular sunrises. A sunset would be more symbolic for a gray voyager, although a sunrise did represent the concept that there could always be a new beginning.

He also fed the numerous deer that roamed the area. He would put out deer corn that he bought by the fifty pound bag at the feed store twice a day on a knoll just up from the cabin, and the deer would come at various times during the day and night. As a special treat he would at times get dropped apples from a nearby orchard and place them among the corn. They were beautiful and graceful animals to watch and study. They knew he would not bother them and even Destiny, who barked at them the first few times she saw them, now only watched them quietly with a particular canine curiosity. He had come a long way from his early days as a city boy. In fact, he had come a long way since he started to look at his life and ascertain its ultimate direction.

Denise stopped by with a peach pie she had baked with his peaches. She told him about an adoption event the animal shelter was going to hold on Saturday accompanied by a craft fair as a fund raiser for the shelter. If Izzy could part with any of his ducks, he could sell them at the fair. They had a folding table and chair as well as a sun tent that he could use, and Lance would take them down to the shelter on Saturday in his truck and put up the tent for him. The ducks were almost like family, but Izzy thought it might prove entertaining to give it a whirl.

On Friday he put in a bin ten ducks that he had chosen in a variety of sizes and colors and encased them in bubble wrap. He made a descriptive card to go along with each duck and set forth a purchase price. He loaded the bin into the truck and sat on the porch with Destiny. He was looking forward to the following day as a new experience. After eighty-five years, one would think there are few new experiences. Yet, when one thinks about it, there are many new things to be exposed to. Newness can be exciting, or at least refreshing, at any age.

Saturday was a beautiful day, and a fairly large crowd showed up at the event. Many people looked at and admired the ducks, and he fielded all sorts of questions. There were only two sales, and he was alright with that joking that the ducks had a long shelf life. In a small way, he was saddened to see the two go.

The highlight of the day was meeting Alexandra Hornfield who captured his interest immediately. It was not only that she was in a wheelchair but there was a striking similarity to Clara, particularly that she seemed to be smiling all of the time. Naturally, she knew all about Izzy, not only because of his legal feats but also because she was on the Board of Directors of the Shelter and Denise had talked about him often. They conversed at length, and Izzy barely noticed the day slip by.

Alexandra was a fascinating person in her own right. As if it were a political statement, she announced that she was three-quarters of a century old and would easily surpass the century mark. As with Izzy, she had been born in New York City, although in Manhattan. Drama was her forte, and she had a successful career on the Broadway stage under the stage name of Xandra Fielding. A serious circulatory infirmity forced her into a wheelchair and an early retirement. She accepted an offer to be the Director of the Asheville Theater Guild because her only daughter was an established artist in the city. Her third husband at the time, who already had a hard time adjusting to her being in a wheelchair, would not leave New York for Asheville. Alexandra, who requested that he call her Alex, had been running the Theater Guild for over twenty years. Since Izzy knew little about the theater except for his college exposure and Alex knew little about ducks, there was much to talk about. Also, she called herself a curbside philosopher and Izzy suspected that would prompt numerous exchanges of wisdom with this intriguing woman.

He certainly was right about that. Extensive nightly telephone calls proved thought-provoking and entertaining. Without a doubt, Alex would be a special friend. For an eighty-five year old man, gaining a new special friend is quite an accomplishment. Maybe, it is a notable accomplishment at any age.

THREE

In one nightly conversation Izzy expounded on the engaging exercise of reviewing childhood memories. At the conclusion, Alex chimed in with a distant tone, "That's all very interesting but pales in comparison when I survey my childhood. There are things I should rightly remember, but I don't. For example, I have absolutely no recollection as a little girl of ever taking a bath. My mother told me she bathed me every night before bedtime except for rare instances when we were out and home too late for the ritual or we had company. So, I have no recollection of an event that evidently was repeated numerous times. How do you account for that?"

"Not sure, although there are many things in the past of every person that were either so common as to be nondescript or just not worth storing in a limited memory bank. Funny you should mention bathing, though. I did not know what hot water was until I went to college. In the apartment in Brooklyn we had sinks in the kitchen and bathroom with a hot water tap and a cold water tap. The hot water taps ran luke warm all year long. The cold water taps ran cold in the winter and warm in the summer. There were times we had no water at all."

Alex sighed. "Today, people are not satisfied even if they have it all."

"That's a fact! A touch of a switch and they have abundant heat or air conditioning. In my building scant heat came up from a coal furnace in the basement only between 7:00 a.m. and 7:00 p.m. if it was running at all."

Alex was silent, and for a moment Izzy thought she had hung up or fallen asleep. He had been known to fall asleep at awkward times, so that possibility could not be ruled out. When she did speak her voice was hushed and barely audible. "Another thing I don't remember is at any time that either my mother or father told me they loved me. They were not affectionate with me or each other." Another period of silence. "I attribute that early absence to my not being able to recognize or give love in my later life. All there was was a series of non-rewarding relationships and failed marriages. A person's course through life can be harsh and down right unfulfilling. I missed out on much that is obvious. I suppose it made me a good actress. I could not live my own life with any success but it was easy to live a scripted existence. The character's emotions and opportunities were preordained."

Izzy knew his best help was just listening, but he also wanted to be supportive. "It is never too late to reach a happy and satisfying place."

"Do you really believe that?"

"I do. I had a loving childhood, a loving marriage, and yet my trip may not be over."

"So, where do you go? What do you do?"

"I have thought about this a lot. Life is a series of destinations. If you reach one that you are content with and it is rewarding does that mean your travel is over? Might be. Might not be."

"They say old people have finished their thinking and living years. You belie that to be merely a stroke of fiction."

"I like to think so."

"So, not too late for me to find love?"

"Absolutely."

"And, my dear shared thinker, what are you after?"

Izzy did not speak for a few seconds. "I still do not know."

FOUR

The conversation the following evening picked up as if the earlier one had not ended. Alex proclaimed, "I am convinced that I should not foreclose any portion of my future. Let me ask you this, once an old person accepts the premise that the journey is not yet over, does he or she have the ability to recognize and act upon a new chapter?"

"An old person, in fact any person, must believe that to achieve the maximum results."

"And, what if fate does not cooperate and in the end there is nothing more?"

"Then, that has to be accepted as well. Yet, believing there is more can bring more."

"And, what if more is merely change?"

"Ah, dear heart, change no matter how slight is a destination, too."

Again Alex was quiet for a few seconds. "I wonder if young people have such pensive moments. I don't remember having any discussions when I was young with friends or adults about chasing a future, defining a destiny or making new paths. I dare say young people are resigned to making do with what comes along. Maybe they are afraid to take an active role for fear of making things worse than they are. My daughter is a talented artist but she leaves her imagination on the canvas. Her day-to-day life is unremarkable, and the relationships she has with her husband and teenaged children are shallow and strained. They react but do not act. Of course, having an invalid in the house with all that demands does not help. I am a depressing element in an already dull existence."

He had not planned on saying it or even had thought about it in advance, but once he said it he was pleased with the thought. "Why don't you come live with me? Lance can build a ramp to the cabin to make it wheelchair accessible."

"An eighty-five year old man cannot, I mean should not, have to handle such a burden."

"Look who is being negative. Perhaps, a life with me in the cabin is your destination."

He could not see the tear descending down her cheek. "Caring for me cannot be your destination."

"Maybe not a final one although I can do it and would like to do it. There are times, as you well know, that things do not become clear until the dust settles."

"To which I add a theatrical line – dust to dust, ashes to ashes."

"Well, what do you think?"

Another tear rolled down her cheek. "I will think about it. I am not so selfish as to answer right away."

"I am selfish enough to hope you will."

FIVE

Three months later Alex moved into Izzy's cabin and remarked how Lance's handiwork had made the entry and exiting easy. The timing was good as winter was about to set in. She had few personal possessions other than clothing, and the guest room closet accommodated the clothing just fine. She proclaimed the guest room was nicer than what she had with her daughter so she was content.

They spent much quiet time reading or watching television, and the atmosphere was relaxed and soothing. although there was no shortage of stimulating conversations. Izzy had found an enjoyment of cooking, and it was no hardship to make extra for Alex although she ate like a bird.

Four days a week he took her to the Theater Guild facility and picked her up at the end of the day, and one day a week it was to the animal shelter. He had plenty of alone time with Destiny who had accepted Alex right away as a member of the family.

One snowy evening, instead of watching television Izzy made a fire in the fireplace and they sat on the sofa before it with Destiny curled up on Izzy's lap. Alex reached for his hand and grasped it firmly. "This is nice. In fact, all of this time with you has been a pleasure."

He returned the pressure on her fingers. "My sentiments exactly."

"Izzy, you are a wonderful man. You are attentive, caring,

and gentle. I get this warm fuzzy feeling all over when I am with you. Tell me, doctor, do you think this is love?"

"Might very well be. The secret is not to question it. Just accept it and bask in it."

"May I sleep with you tonight? If I hold you, the reality will set in."

"I would enjoy that."

He leaned towards her and they kissed tenderly. Youth may have added passion in their embraces, but the embers burn warm and steady for those of advanced years.

Izzy awoke early as was his habit. Alex's arm was wrapped around him and her head was on his chest. Her sleep was peaceful. He thought to himself that they had reached a mutual destination. Two people, particularly elderly people, reach a point of serene contentment when they share a meaningful companionship so whatever days remain in the total life journey are not spent alone. He should have figured it out before this that a final destination would be relatively uncomplicated. Even if a Hollywood version would make sure it was grandiose and monumental, reality ushers forth the beauty and deeper meaning of a simple place. It is the knowing that this is where he needed to be, where he wanted to be. Even if nothing exists beyond that, in good conscience the hot air balloon can be tethered and no further flights undertaken.